For Ben,
thank you for all
your support.
CA

LiTTLE TiGER
LONDON

LITTLE TIGER
An imprint of Little Tiger Press Limited
www.littletiger.co.uk
1 Coda Studios, 189 Munster Road, London SW6 6AW
Imported into the EEA by Penguin Random House Ireland,
Morrison Chambers, 32 Nassau Street, Dublin D02 YH68
First published in Great Britain 2022
This edition published in 2023
Text and illustration copyright © Clara Anganuzzi 2022
A CIP catalogue record for this book is available from the British Library
All rights reserved • Printed in China
ISBN: 978-1-83891-514-8
CPB/1400/2282/1022
10 9 8 7 6 5 4 3 2 1

The Forest Stewardship Council® (FSC®) is an international,
non-governmental organisation dedicated to promoting
responsible management of the world's forests. FSC®
operates a system of forest certification and product
labelling that allows consumers to identify wood
and wood-based products from well-managed
forests and other controlled sources.

For more information about the FSC®,
please visit their website at www.fsc.org

There is more than one way to be...

STRONG

Written and illustrated by
Clara Anganuzzi

What do you know about dragons?

They are **mighty**
and ferocious.

They like to snarl and growl.

They are **tough**
and **powerful**.

But, hold on –
you don't know **everything**
about dragons because you
haven't met Maurice yet...

Maurice is not your average dragon.
He is small, gentle and quiet.

Oh, and he **absolutely adores flowers!**

Maurice loves diving into seas of colours and smells,
where he can look for the perfect red hibiscus
or the largest, happiest sunflowers.

With these, Maurice likes
to weave and sculpt beautiful
flower arrangements.

The other dragons aren't interested in flowers.

They have far more 'dragonly' things to do,
such as breathing fire and winning competitions!
Every year, the dragons gather to find out
who is the strongest of them all.

The winner is usually Gruff.
He is Maurice's brother.

Gruff is large,
rough and loud
(and he definitely
doesn't have time
for flowers).

Blazing
bursts of
flames
are one of his
specialities!

This is Maurice's first contest!

He is captivated by Gruff's fiery shapes, and he wonders if he can create his own glorious hibiscus flower.

Maurice takes a big breath in,
and then stops…

Gruff's flames have left
paths of scorched flowers.

So, instead of a **huge**
blaze of fire, Maurice
just lets out a
little puff.

The next stage of the contest is the scaring round.

The dragons bare their **sharp** teeth,

stretch their *pointed wings*

and parade their
magnificent
horns.

It seems that however hard Maurice tries,
he never **quite** manages to fit in.

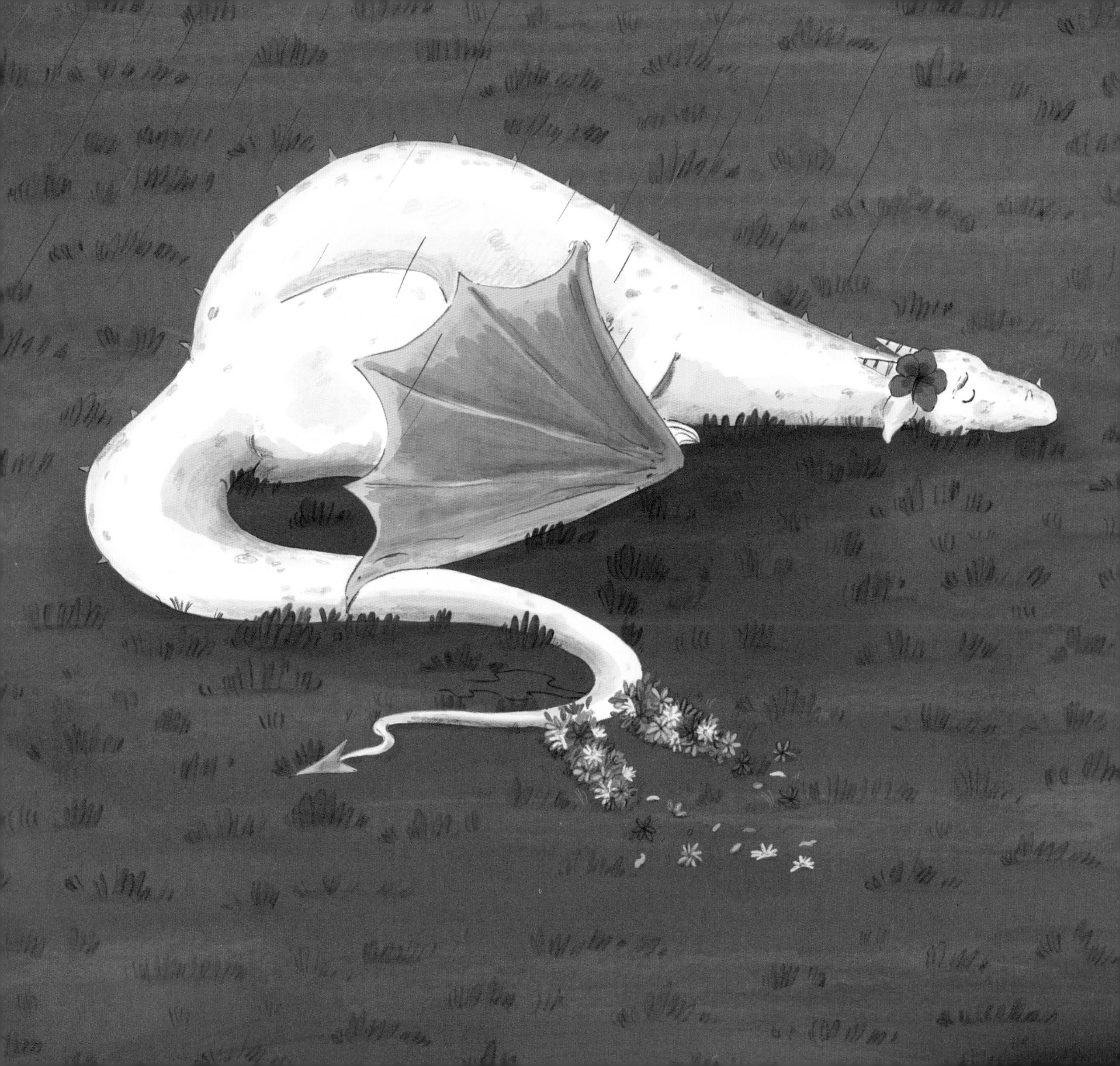

Gentle drops of rain begin to run off
Maurice's scales as he lies down with a sigh.

I'm not strong or brave or scary,
and I don't like breathing fire.
I'll never be like the other dragons.

The drizzle quickens and a **storm** starts to brew.

The final round of the competition is the famous gold treasure hunt,
but the snaps and crackles in the sky make Maurice feel nervous.

Maybe we should go on our hunts in the morning instead?

Gruff disagrees.
He wants to defend his title as reigning champion.

You'll never be a strong dragon if you don't try, Maurice!

Gruff puffs out his chest and flies up high into the dark clouds.

The storm rages on and on,
and the dragons begin to worry.

What is taking
Gruff so long?

Perhaps he's hurt.
We should find him!

But what if
we all get lost?

Maurice quietly fidgets with his daisy garland until... I have an idea!

Up the dragons fly
in a **daisy-chain**
formation with
little Maurice
in the lead.

The dragons swoop high and low until they find Gruff, but his wing is hurt. How will they ever get him home?

While the others gather around Gruff, Maurice spots a willow tree and dashes off.

What **are** you doing, Maurice?

Put those twigs down and help us!

But Maurice **is** helping!

Using his floristry skills, Maurice criss-crosses, zigzags and weaves the bendy branches

tightly together until he has made a willow harness the perfect size for Gruff!

When the dragons return home safely,
everyone cheers for Maurice!

Maurice blushes as he looks at the happy faces — it is as if they are seeing him for the first time.

As the daisies close
their petals for the night,
there is one thing left
for Gruff to do.

I thought there was only one way
to be strong, but I was wrong,
Maurice. Your strength comes
from being true to yourself.

Maurice thinks about the delicate
flowers that grow among rocks,
quietly and boldly breaking
through.

And, at last,
he realises that
he has **always**
been **strong.**

So, now you really do know
everything about dragons...

Sometimes they breathe
flames, but sometimes
they breathe flowers.